SHE
THE SHAMELESS WIFE

VIDUSHI GUPTA

ISBN 979-888521806-1

Dedicated to all the wives of India living inabusive marriages.

Contents

Contents

Anu was sitting very still on the balcony of her flat, watching the ever-busy roads of Mumbai from the fifteenth floor of her building. The sun was setting down somewhere in the Arabian sea, just like, according to her, her life was setting down and it was entering into a mode of darkness. She threw a glance over her wrist and found finger impressions there. Then she gently touched her swollen and bitten lips; they hurt. Her wounds were reminding her what she wanted to forget; last night. And not just that one night, she wanted to forget her whole marriage which was turning out to be the worst ever mistake of her life.

"What's wrong love?" Karan, her husband came and sat beside her, concern in his voice.

Anu stayed silent. Two years of a relationship and four years of marriage with this man, and she still could not believe she had made a terrible mistake. She looked at him before answering, but she found no guilt at all. "Beautiful sunset, isn't it?" He asked again without noticing that she hadn't even replied to his first question. This was the thing that Anu, in their four years of marriage had noticed about Karan, He was always living in his mind oblivious to what and how she felt about things, for him, only his side of the story mattered. He questioned her often about things, trying to show that he cared about her, but then he moved on without listening to her reply. She again studied his face, short army cut hair, slight stubble on a dusky oval-shaped face, transparent spectacles. A very average Indian man. Who could tell that this man could have the ability to abuse his wife, to cheat on her and have an extra-marital affair, to be oblivious to his little daughter?

"Anu, why are you so quiet? Look at the sunset, so romantic." Karan finally turned towards her and looked into her eyes, holding her hands, repeating his sentence.

"Ouch." Anu grimaced as he held her wrist on the same point he had given her a bruise.

"Ohh, I am sorry." Karan apologized and started his inspection of her wounds.

"Nothing too serious. They will heal within a week, don't worry." He said finally.

"That is if you won't give me any new ones, on my body, heart, or soul." Anu taunted. It was totally beyond her that how can Karan be so normal, so guilt-free even after raising his hand on her. There wasn't a bit of sorry written on the face, in his eyes, or his body language.

"Why do you say things like these Anu? This is exactly why it happens. Why do you anger me with your words? I try so hard to be a good husband, but you always make it so hard." He talked through gritted teeth.

"Good husband? What you did with me last night is called domestic violence and marital rape Karan. Does it sound like something a good husband would do? You're having an extramarital affair with your colleague, is that something a good husband would do?" Anu questioned Karan very politely without raising her voice, but her eyes were full of tears. She felt broken, her soul felt crushed, and she wanted to drown deep down in tears of pain. She wanted to yell that she was tired and that she was done taking all the abuse for years. That she was so done with all of it. "Nonsense. What do you mean by domestic violence and marital rape? Come on Anu, a slap here and there doesn't mean I am torturing you. And marital rape? Seriously? You're my wife. My wife. There is no such thing as marital rape between a husband and a wife. All this stupid feminism has gone to your head. Also, I am not having an affair with anyone." Karan replied. He wasn't shouting, but his voice was indeed loud enough to wake up their two-year-old daughter. Anu's head was feeling heavy. She wasn't able to comprehend what this man, the man she loved once, the man she had married was saying to her face. She couldn't fathom the sexism and lying coming out of his mouth. "Yes, you're. I have gone through your phone calls, pictures, and messages, and I know what all is being exchanged." Anu got up to go and fend for her baby. It was time to feed her.

"What did you say? Did you go through my phone? You spied on me?" Karan almost shouted in anger this time and Anu ignored him. She went into her room and picked up Kia who was crying hysterically.

"Mumma is here baby, stop crying." Anu embraced Kia and wiped her tears and coddled her protectively.

"What did you say there?" Karan followed Anu in the room, shouting again. Anu could see his wrists clenching. A part of her was afraid of the man who was standing in front of her as she didn't want any more bruises.

"Don't shout, Kia is here too."

"I don't care. Your daughter has nothing else to do apart from crying."

"My daughter?" Anu was flabbergasted. If anything, more than anger, she was beginning to foster the feeling of fear and hatred for the man standing in front of her.

Karan remained silent.

"She's your daughter too, in case you're forgetting." She spoke through clenched teeth.

"Whatever Anu, I don't care! You stay away from my privacy and do not ever touch my phone again, no matter what."

With that, Karan stormed off from the room, leaving his crying wife and daughter behind.

"Karan, I want to talk with you about something."

It was a normal Sunday afternoon. Karan was watching something on his phone, Kia was playing on the floor and Anu was mindlessly staring at the ceiling fan after finishing her household chores.

"Hmm?" He said without looking up from his phone.

"Karan, can you give me your undivided attention for five minutes?" Anu sighed, trying hard not to pick up a fight again.

"Sure." Karan finally put down his phone and turned towards his wife. "Tell me."

"Karan, I feel bored at home. I mean, before marriage, I was working, I was independent, I was doing something I loved, but these days, all my time is invested in changing diapers and cleaning milk bottles and scrubbing kitchen counters." Anu spoke in a breath and then stopped for her husband to say something.

He remained silent.

"What? I thought you were not done." He finally spoke.

"Karan, I want to resume work." She sighed again, making her point clear.

"What? Why?" He gave a reaction like she had asked him to give her a kidney.

"I just told you why."

"You want to resume work because you're bored with taking care of our family?" Karan spoke in an accusing tone.

"No, I did not mean it like that."

"You did. If you'll go to work, who will look after our home, our daughter?" He interrupted.

"Karan, Kia is almost three now. We can keep her in playschool or daycare. We can even take her to our workplaces, most of them offer in house spaces for kids now and there are people there who look after them. We can manage."

"Acha. And what about home? Who will look after it? Who will cook?" Karan was visibly irritated by now.

"We can hire a maid. We live in a two BHK flat, it's not too huge, I can easily manage it and even you could lend me a hand if things got too messy." Anu tried to reason with her husband, even when she could tell she was fighting a lost battle.

"So now you want to say I am keeping you in a small house, but also want me to help you around it?"

"No Karan, why can't you understand, it's not about you or Kia, it's about me, my dreams, my freedom, and aspirations."

Anu was horrified. What was she saying and what was he understanding. "Absolutely what I am saying Anu, you're only thinking about yourself, not about me or Kia. When other women can give up their careers for their husbands and family, why can't you? What is the big deal?" Karan was losing his temper minute by minute.

"I don't care about what other women are doing, I care about what I want to do."

Anu had tried hard to contain her temper, but after listening to what Karan had to say, her voice was rising. "You're not going to do any job. You're going to look after our home. Kia is turning three now, we should start planning for another child. It's the correct time, even my family was telling me to try for a baby boy this time around. You'll also have something to look forward to." Karan got up, stretched his hands in a way to show that he has told his final decision and no further discussion would be held on it. Anu saw him leaving and then resumed staring at the ceiling. her eyes watering.

"Mummmmaaa....don'tttt cryyy..." Kia, who was silently watching her parents argue, came near her mother to wipe her tears when her father left without paying any attention to them.

"I love you, my baby." Anu smiled and hugged her little daughter, touched by her love. Kia was just a child, still was so sensitive about her mother's feelings. Karan was a fully grown man and yet was so oblivious to his wife's emotions.

III

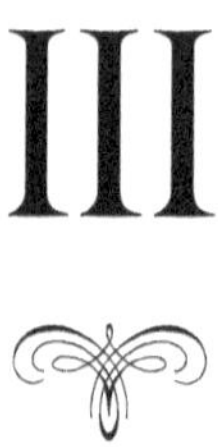

"Anu, how are you doing?"

Anu was talking to her mother on a phone call after two weeks. In some past months, she had reduced communicating with her parents, afraid that she might worry them even more.

"I am fine Ma."

"You don't sound fine to me." Her mother retorted.

Anu smiled humorlessly. Mothers cannot hide anything from them. Especially sadness. They have radar to find out when their children are going through something hard, even if they're thousands of miles away.

"Sometimes Ma, I think I committed a huge mistake by marrying Karan. I think I should have listened to you and Papa."

"Has anything happened? Did he hit you again?" This time, Ma was gentler and more worried.

"A few days ago. A slap." Anu, at this point, was sobbing.

"What can I say beta, Karan wasn't like this at all. I and your father were against this marriage, but it was for other reasons. We never thought even in our wildest dreams that Karan could do such things." Anu could hear her mother's voice breaking on the other end. This was exactly why she didn't want to tell things to her parents.

"But he did turn out to be like this Ma." Anu wiped her tears.

"Anu, beta, now you're married, you have a daughter."

"I don't know what you want to say Ma."

"Sometimes, as women, we have to adjust to save our homes Anu. Sometimes we have to let things go."

"Ma, you also know it is not the first time he had hit me."

"I know. But look at the good things. He does so much for you. Your home has everything. He has bought everything for you Anu. It's not like he's keeping you badly."

"So you are saying I should go on living like this? That somehow, a roof, a television, an air conditioner, or food is enough compensation for him to abuse me like this." Anu was flabbergasted.

"I am not saying anything Anu. God knows I want you to be happy. I want Karan to give you all the love and respect. But he isn't giving any of this at the point. And we are getting old. How can I tell you to leave him? If you leave him, if you'll come back, how will we support you and Kia? She needs her father, you need a husband in this society."

"So is it only us who needs him? Doesn't he need us too?"

"He does, but you need him more. He's a man, you both are women."

By this moment, Anu was so irritated with her mother, she just wanted to hang up straight, but she controlled herself. What was it with everyone around her turning up so sexist and misogynist all of a sudden?

"Maa, Kia is up, I will call you back in sometime."

Before her mother could give her any reply, Anu had disconnected the call already, had disconnected from the conversation, and was lost in her thoughts.

IV

"Hey, can you pack my stuff? I am going for a three day trip with my office colleagues tomorrow."

Anu was serving Karan his plate of breakfast, but when she heard him, she stopped midway.

"Three day trip with your office mates?" She asked with disappointing anticipation.

"Yes. We are all going to Goa, it's a long weekend." He replied, tearing a piece of omelet with his knife and fork.

"But Karan, if you have three days off, you, I, and Kia can go somewhere. I haven't gone out of Mumbai for a year." Anu suggested hoping Karan would for once, do something to make her happy.

Karan looked at her with disbelief in his eyes.

"I cannot believe this Anu. Every time I want to do something for myself, you always put yourself and Kia in between." His voice was full of rude accusation.

"Karan, even I put you and our daughter above myself. You said you don't want me to go for a job, I obliged. Now if I am telling you to spend some days with your wife and daughter, what is the big deal?"

Karan was agitated, his temper rising.

"I spend so much time with you two. Whatever I am doing, earning, I am doing for you both. Can't I simply spend a few days with my friends alone?" He shouted.

"Since when your office colleagues are your friends? And don't I get equally tired and bored of living in the house and doing chores for you and Kia? Don't I have feelings? Can I not want to simply go somewhere and relax for a few days?"

"Then go by yourself with your friends, I am not taking you, and in anyways, what do you even do sitting in his house other than leeching off my hard-earned money?" Karan started buttering a piece of bread.

"Is she going too?" Anu asked slowly. Though her heart was pierced by his last statement, she chose to ignore it.

"Who she?" Karan asked, taking a sip from his juice.

"You know who I am talking about."

Karan threw the bread on the floor.

"For heaven's sake Anu, nothing is going on between me and Ritu. We are simply colleagues and friends at most. You don't even let me eat two morsels of food peacefully in this house. To hell with you. I am leaving. No need to pack anything, I would go directly"

Anu, once again, simply watched like a mute spectator as her husband left the house for his vacation for a few days.

It was eleven at the night. Kia was in deep sleep and Anu was sitting on their desk, a book in front of her. Karan hadn't given her a call since he had left the house. She had texted him but to no avail. He hadn't replied, he hadn't even seen the texts. Maybe he was having fun with his friends in Goa whereas she was alone, sulking. She decided to video call her friend Chavi. Anu and Chavi had met each other in-office parties as Ashwin, Chavi's husband and Karan were colleagues and very soon the four had become good friends.

"She must be feeling off too as Ashwin must have gone with Karan. Let me call her, might be we both can do a night over."

Anu thought and dialed Chavi's number. After a few rings, Ashwin picked up the call.

"Hey Anu, how are you? Chavi is in the washroom. All good?" He said with a smiling face.

"Hi, Ashwin." Anu was surprised to see Ashwin at home, "Did you not go with Karan on the office trip?"

Now it was Ashwin who made a puzzled face.

"Which office trip?" He asked.

"Arey, that office trip to Goa na."

"Anu, I am very active in the office but there is no office trip to Goa or anywhere. However, on this long weekend, I and Chavi are going to Lonavala. We will simply drop the kids at my parents' house for a couple of days. It's been so long I and Chavi had been somewhere alone." He said, his face and voice beaming with excitement.

"Ohh. I think I must have heard it wrong." Anu replied, her mind already registering the possibility of the worst.

"Maybe. Hey, Chavi is here....."

Before Ashwin could've finished his sentences, Anu had disconnected the call.

Anu stared long at her phone's screen. There still was no reply from Karan, and her heart sank at the thought of her worst fears coming to life finally.

V

Anu was sitting in the hall. It was two in the morning. She had called Karan fifty times, and not once he answered the call. She had called most of his teammates who she thought could've accompanied Karan to the office trip, if there was even a real official trip to begin with, who were all however in their houses with their families, and that deepened her suspicion. Interestingly, when she had called Ritu, again the call went unanswered, and the second time, it was switched off. Anu was in her thirties, she was a well-educated woman who had worked for quite a long period in her life.

Long story short, she was not a person who lacked the brains to put two plus two.

Her husband was on a trip with another woman.

Her husband was cheating on her.

Anu stood up and went to the bar cabinet. She poured herself a glass of wine, came back to her seat, and then played her favorite song on the music system. An eerie sense of calm came around her once she realized she was being cheated on, and that her marriage was finally over.

"Lag ja gale, ki fir yeh, hasi raat ho na ho..
Shayad fir iss janam mai, mulakaat ho na ho..."

Anu was humming the complete song, singing along the lines, sipping on her favorite white wine, scrolling through their family pictures in her phone, looking at the pictures she and Karan had taken- before their marriage, after their marriage, when she was pregnant, when Kia was born. They were their 'Happy pictures'.

There were very fewer moments Anu was really happy after she had married Karan, and those few ones were captured on camera as memories.

She sipped on some more wine, restarted the song, and began thinking about how it all began. Her story with Karan, the way they had met, it was the first day of her office. Her marriage with Karan.

Anu closed her eyes, trying to think where she had gone wrong, where the marriage had gone wrong. The early days of their relationship were good, they had gone through so much together to get married as both of them belonged to different castes.

Maybe it all started after the first few days of marriage when they had both started living with Karan's family and there were frequent fights. Or maybe it all started when Karan took a job in a new city to give his marriage with Anu another chance with no heart. Or maybe it all started when Anu had delivered a baby girl instead of a baby boy, or maybe the lack of quality and frequent sex led to all of this.

Anu took a long drag of her drink; finishing it. Her head was spinning and she felt she was going to throw up. But not so soon, she thought to herself. Not before she knew where her marriage was so damned that it came to all of this.

VI

Six years ago. Anu was almost running into her office. She was trying hard to balance between her purse, her lunch box, her ID card, her hairs simply sticking on her sweaty face out from her loosely tied bun. Her flats were giving her a nightmare, she hadn't anticipated her first day in her first job would be so tedious.

"Hey, you need any help?" A guy, barely in her mid-twenties asked her from somewhere behind.

Anu turned around and saw this tall, dusky-skinned, lean guy, all dressed in a white shirt and grey trousers. He had long hairs for a normal Indian guy, his locks falling freely on his forehead, giving him a rather shabby look, his shirt's sleeves were rolled up to his elbows. All in all, a guy Anu could think of befriending on the first day itself. He seemed sweet in his first impression rather than intimidating.

"Are you okay?" He came closer and asked again.

"Yeah, it's just that it's my first day at my first job. I guess I am nervous." Anu smiled nervously, and it was true, her stomach was filled with thousands of butterflies.

"Don't be." The guy smiled too.

"I am a bit late today. I just hope my team leader is not some strict oldie."

"What's your name?" The guy tried to peek in her ID.

"Anu Garg."

The guy started laughing.

"Lovely and interesting coincidence." He said, holding his laughter.

"I am sorry, I didn't get you. Why are you laughing?"

"Hi, I am Karan Singh, your team leader. And I am not a strict and oldie TL at all." He smiled mischievously.

Anu's mouth fell open.

"You're my team leader?" She was bewildered.

"Why? Can't I be?"

"No, I mean yes, you can be. But how did you recognize me?"

Karan smiled, warmer this time.

"I got a mail detailing about a few new trainees who will be joining today, and your name was in that list."

"Ohh."

"Yes."

Suddenly, it struck Anu that she was standing in front of her immediate 'boss', sending a wave of terror on her face.

"I am so sorry Sir, I didn't want to be late on the first day itself, but I am new to this city, and I got stuck in traffic and all, I promise it won't happen again." She spoke like a child who has been caught doing something naughty.

"Anu, relax. It's okay."

"I am so sorry Sir, I am a punctual person."

"Anu, I said it happens." Karan was a little loud this time, but still polite. "And please don't call me Sir. I must be just a couple of years elder than you. Call me Karan."

Anu simply nodded, her face showing all shades of excitement, terror and relief, all at once. "Are you okay?"

He smiled brightly and asked her once again flashing his charming smile.

Anu nodded again.

"Chalo then, let's go, we both have work to do."

Anu silently nodded for the third time and followed Karan without protesting, something she was going to do for years that were yet to come.

VII

"Hey Anu, what are you doing?"

Anu was simply initiating her break after an extremely draining client call from the US when she felt Karan beside her.

"Nothing Karan. I was just going to grab a bite. Some clients are a pure headache."

"Oh, that's correct, I agree." Karan nodded," Do you mind if I join you?"

Anu looked at him skeptically, she wanted to have her food in some peace, maybe listen to her music and unwind, but how could she say no to him? He was her team leader and maybe he could've taken it otherwise.

"Of course. Let's go."

Karan and Anu were sitting in the office cafeteria. Karan was eating a sandwich while Anu was having a light fruit salad.

"You're only having fruits?" Karan signaled to Anu's plate full of fruit pieces.

"Yes, I like having fruits in the afternoon. They're very healthy and refreshing."

"Ohh. No wonder you look so fit and energetic." He complimented.

Anu blushed. " Thanks, Karan."

"From tomorrow, you and I will have lunch together and you must remind me to have only fruits at lunch just like yourself. Even I want to be fit and fine and healthy, just like you." He spoke enthusiastically.

"Okay, done." Anu laughed and agreed, finally feeling at ease.

"So Anu, what more do you like, you know, apart from eating fruits," Karan asked while resuming gobbling on his chicken sandwich.

"I like reading a lot, and music, and cooking. These three hobbies, I love them." She stabbed a piece of apple with her fork while answering.

"Hey, I like cooking too." Karan was pleasantly surprised.

"Hello, fellow foodie." Anu smiled widely. It was true that she was fond of food, both cooking and eating different cuisines and dishes made her heart lose all its pain for the time being.

"I feel the same."

Anu nodded, stabbing a strawberry this time.

"Hey, if you don't mind, can I ask you a question."

Anu stopped chewing at this for a moment. She had lived enough to know that when people usually asked permission before asking a question, it meant the question had to be personal. She was also wise to realize that every statement that started with "No offense" was again, almost always offensive.

"Sure, go ahead." She was skeptical, but still all geared up for what was coming next.

"Do you have a boyfriend?" Karan asked sheepishly.

Anu stared at him for a while, deciding what to answer, but then she went ahead with the truth.

"I had one for five years, but we broke up a few months back."

"Ohh, that's extremely sad."

"Hmm. It just didn't work out. We both wanted different things from life, so we called it off amicably. One of the reasons why I came to a new city. To have a fresh start in my life."

"That's a commendable thought Anu. You did it right. Life must move on."

"What about you Karan? Any girlfriend?" Anu tossed the question back at him while mouthing the final fruit of the plate.

Karan also took the last bite of his sandwich before answering.

"Had quite a few, but none lasted too long. Guess hadn't stumbled upon Ms. Right till now." He winked.

Anu blushed again.

"So what's your definition of Ms. Right?"

Karan kept his face on his hands, pretending to think.

"I am a simple guy Anu. I just want a girl who can respect me, understand me, support me, and gel with my family. That is it."

"Interesting. Who's in your family?"

"Grandparents, parents, an elder married brother with kids and two younger sisters. A simple joint family and we all live in the same house in this city."

Anu took a sip of water on the statement. All the subtle flirting took the backseat. A simple joint family? Was he kidding? As per her maths, not that she was good at it, but still, according to her calculations, there were eleven members in his family including him.

"Hello? Miss lost?" Karan shook her a little, and Anu was back in the conversation.

"Sorry, I just zoned out."

"Where to?"

Anu made a poker face before answering. How could she put up such a personal and sensitive statement as an answer?

"I was just thinking that you have a joint family."

"So?" Suddenly Karan was even more interested in the conversation.

"Isn't that a bit hard? To live amongst so many people?"

Karan shrugged.

"That's how I have been living since childhood you know. So I don't feel much of a problem. Besides, there are so many people that I never feel alone, you know, there's always someone I can talk to. There's nothing else more important to me than all of them. Festivals and weddings are so awesome, you should attend something like that in my house."

Anu moved her neck up and down. So what if he had a large family, it's not like they were getting married. Nothing was going on between them even, then why was she even bothered about imagining to be a part of his family. She took a sip of water and stood up before the conversation took another personal turn.

"Alright Karan, the break is over. I got to be back at my desk. You know my team leader is a very strict man." She said in a teasing manner.

"Ohh, is that so? Then I suggest you leave quickly before he fires you." Karan stood up too and winked playfully.

"Ahh, I am afraid he cannot fire me."

"And why do you think that?"

Anu signaled Karan to lend his ear to her. He bowed down a bit and placed his ear near her face. She shifted towards him, stood a little on her toes, brought her lips near

to his ears, and whispered.
"Because I know he likes me."

VIII

A few months passed. The things in the office were stable. People were doing their job, people were being hired, people were being fired, a few of them resigning from their jobs, then there were office parties and trips and bonuses and appraisals and promotions and transfers. All in all, everything was normal for Anu in her office, apart from this one thing- She and Karan were getting closer to each other day by day. The shared lunches and conversations, the stolen glances, the innocent physical touches, the soft giggling, and the thrill of having a mutual attraction.

"Hey, Anu."

On one fine weekend, Anu's phone beeped and a message from Karan popped up on her screen. She was reading a recipe book when the phone's sound disturbed her.

"Hello, Karan."

"What are you doing?" He texted back almost immediately.

"Nothing much. You say?" She typed back quickly too.

"Well, I was wondering if you're free tomorrow, why don't we go and catch a movie or something?" His message, again, came quickly.

"Oh, who else is going?" She typed, suppressing a lazy yawn.

"Noone. It's just you and me." This time, the reply was a bit delayed by a few seconds, as if he had taken his time to type the sentence.

"Are you asking me out on a date?" Now the conversation had her interest.

"Yes."

"Hmm. Okay. Let's go." She smiled broadly while typing.

"So it's a date?" He sent in with heart emojis.

"Yes, it is. A date. Tomorrow at five. Our first date."

Anu was waiting for Karan to pick her up from her PG. She was wearing a tucked in red shirt, blue jeans, and very light makeup of some simple foundation, some kohl, and lip-gloss. Anu had never felt the need of filling her face with different colors, her face wasn't a drawing or coloring book for her. No matter the occasion, her makeup was always extremely minimal.

"Hey Sorry, got a bit late. Traffic is really bad. Come on hop on quickly else we will miss the beginning of the movie." Karan started speaking as soon as stopped his bike in front of her.

Anu sat behind Karan, close enough to rest her head on his shoulder. She felt warmth, security, and most importantly, love.

They watched a movie, had a proper candlelight dinner, and when Karan had asked Anu if she would like to be his girlfriend when he was dropping ger off in front of her building's gate, she had said yes without waiting for a moment. And then she had danced her heart off when she was back in her room with her friends. She was in love with Karan, and he was in love with her.

IX

Months passed. Anu and Karan were now in a relationship. The time when a relationship starts, the earliest months of any relationship, the honeymoon period, as they say, is one of the most beautiful periods a couple spends together and the same was true for them both. Every day they were meeting and spending their time with each other in the office. On weekends, they had their movies, shopping, outings, lunch, and dinner dates. In the nights, they were texting and calling each other all the time. All in all, Anu was living a fairy tale life. After her break-up ten months ago, she had left any hope of finding love ever again, but she had found it in Karan rather quickly.

Nine months passed into their relationship. It was Sunday. Anu and Karan were sitting in a cafe that day, having coffee and some fries. Karan was visibly nervous that day as if something was bothering him. Rather than sipping on his coffee and having a romantic chat with his girlfriend, he was sitting silently

"Is something wrong Karan? Did I do something wrong?" She asked.

"Nope."

"Then what is it? You can tell me." She reached across the table and held Karan's hand.

Karan looked up at her, in her eyes, and kept his other hand on her hand.

"I am already going in my late twenties now Anu, and my parents and the whole family are pressurizing me to get married."

Anu's face went cold. Marriage? Where did that come from?

"So what is your stand?" She asked him in a stunned tone, not missing the slight hint of fear in her voice.

"Of course I want to marry you. I want to tell them about us."

"Ohh."

Karan moved from his chair to the other one that was nearer to Anu.

"Anu, I am nervous because I have never asked this question to another girl."

Anu knew what was coming next, and inside her heart, she was already ready with her answer.

"Miss Anu Garg, will you marry me?"

Anu was in shock, though a pleasant one. She looked at Karan and went through their time together. Six months of flirting and then nine months of a relationship that was full of ups and downs. Karan was a dominant guy, possessive, a bit jealous. But then, this was the case with every other guy out there. Anu had seen men with worse habits. Men are like that, she had thought in her mind. But Karan, he just had a very few drawbacks, he was in Anu's eyes much better than other men. She wanted to spend her life with him, she was sure. He was the perfect guy for her, the guy who was taking a stand for her in front of his family. What more proof a girl needs from a guy about the trueness of his love?

"Speak na Anu, will you marry me?" Karan asked again, with a softer and more hopeful voice.

"Yes Karan, I will marry you," Anu replied with a shy smile and excited voice.

"Really?"

Anu nodded her head.

"Yes, she said yes!" Suddenly Karan jumped with joy and started shouting at the top of his lungs. Everyone who was sitting inside the café started looking at him like he was crazy, but Karan had no care about the world. He was jumping and dancing and giggling in joy.

Anu joined him too, something inside her telling that she had made the right choice. At least she hoped she had. After all, what could be better than marrying the one you love and spending the rest of your life with them?

X

"No, no, no Anu, we cannot marry you to that boy. We just cannot."

"But why Papa, what is the problem? He is educated, he comes from a good family, he is good looking and he earns quite decent. He is a hard-working guy, he and I will manage things."

"No Anu, you're not understanding. We have met him and his family, and even if we keep the matter of different castes aside, I and your mother don't think you'll be happy in this marriage." He threw a glance at his wife.

"I am turning twenty-six this year, and do you guys think I am a fool to choose Karan?" Anu almost shouted in anger.

"Don't shout in front of your father Anu." This time, it was Anu's mother who chided her," Your father and I think you won't be able to adjust in his family, we are a nuclear family and he has what, around eleven members?"

Anu was feeling the heat in her facial muscles, but she also did not want to make things worse by having a heated argument with her parents because at the end of the day she needed them to marry Karan. She couldn't marry without her parent's blessings. She took a long breath, calmed herself down, and then looked at her parents with pleading eyes because she knew they always worked.

"Please Mom, please Papa, I love him, and he loves me too. I know he has a vast family but they are all good people. I know I will adjust there in no time."

"We want to marry you in this city itself Anu, you'll be near to us." Her mother ruffled her hair, worry clear in her eyes for her daughter's future.

"I know Mom, but Delhi isn't too far. I will come down to meet you guys every month I promise." She pleaded again.

Anu's parents looked at each other. Both were in their early fifties, both had seen their share of lives to realize that what Anu was asking would, more probably than not bring certain miseries, and like every set of parents, they were trying hard to save their daughter from any sort of pains.

"Anu, we just are not getting good vibes out of it." Her mother tried to reason with her daughter again.

"Maa, Papa, alright, if you both are so adamant, I will not marry Karan."

"Anu? That is what we are telling you. Don't worry, I'll find the perfect boy for my daughter." Her father said in a happy tone.

"Let me finish my sentence, Papa. I said I won't marry Karan because I don't want to hurt you two, but also, I love Karan, and I cannot cheat him by marrying someone else, so I'll remain unmarried." Anu declared in a determined tone.

"Anu, what are you saying?"

"Yes Maa, I won't marry anyone else. You said no to Karan, and I respect your decision. Now I am saying no for other guys, so I expect you both to respect my decision too."

Anu, after her final declaration, stood up and finally went to her room. Emotional blackmailing was her last resort against her parents, something she knew that has always worked, whether it was the college trip or joining the job in another city, and she had a hinge that it would work this time again.

And she was right. Two days later, Karan was sitting in her home with his parents for finalizing their marriage.

XI

Anu's and Karan's wedding was like a war fought in itself. Family on both sides made it quite sure to show at every step how unhappy they were of the union, and how forced it all was. To make the matters worse, both sides left no stone unturned to break into constant disagreements because of cultural differences. When the wedding was finally over, Karan and Anu had felt like soldiers who have just returned from a bloody battle. "Let's pack our bags fast and leave for our honeymoon." Karan had said to Anu after a week of their marriage.

"True that. I cannot wait to get away from all this drama for a few days." She had replied. They had gone to Bali for two weeks. Those fourteen days have been some of the best days of her life. After a crazy wedding, the honeymoon came like magic. "While we were getting married, in all these months, we have fought so much with each other because of our families," Anu whispered into Karan's ear. They both were lying naked on the bed after making love, gazing into the night sky.

"Yes, there were so many times I wondered if they were right that we both weren't meant to be with each other." His voice was soft too.

"Once or twice even I contemplated calling the wedding off just to be at peace," Anu replied, her eyes lost somewhere far in the sky.

"Thank God you didn't call it off, else how could this particular moment have been possible, huh?"

He brought her close and kissed her on the lips.

"Yes, thank God I decided to marry a total nutcase like you, else you would have remained unmarried forever." She teased him.

"Acha, you think I would have never married if you would have said no?" He faked some anger.

"No, I didn't say that. I simply meant that no girl would have said yes, you know, not every girl is mad like me." She teased him again and they both broke into musical laughter before starting their next passionate session of love and lust. Anu was happy in the arms of the man she loved and desired, knowing in the heart that this man would fill her life with happiness and love.

At that moment, there wasn't any soul on earth who was happier than Anu.

But very soon, this was going to change.

One year later.

They say that fairy tales end at 'they lived happily ever after', and real tales begin at, 'the reality begins after marriage.' After a year of being married to Karan and his family, yes, according to Anu, it was not just Karan she had married, but his whole family, she had concluded that her life was in a hot mess.

At first, she was told to leave her job for some time. When she looked back at it all, she knew it started then.

"You can rejoin in some company after a year or so once you get settled in your new life here. Till then you just get to know all my family members and have fun." Karan had said to her a few days later after their return from honeymoon.

And she had mindlessly obliged. She had thought about what harm could it do to enjoy her new life for some time, and later she can always return to her job. Plus managing new responsibilities with a career could've been a headache.

Slowly and steadily, Anu tried hard to mix in, but no matter how hard she tried, due to the obvious differences, she would always feel the odd one out in the huge family. At first, almost everyone was helpful and supportive, but after seeing Anu fail repeatedly, the other family members, even Karan's disdain was growing towards her. It was beginning to dawn on her what her parents had told her before marriage. No matter how hard she tried, her ways were almost always colliding with Karan's family. "Why can't you wake at five like my mother ask you to?" He would complain.

"Because I sleep at two in the morning." She would shout back.

"Why can't you simply follow what my parents ask you to?" He would say in anger.

"Can you live your life according to my parent's wish? If not, how can you ask me to completely change myself as per your parent's wishes?" She would retort.

"I am a man, you're a woman. It is you who needs to adjust according to me and my family. We live in India, this is how is it here." He would scream and go out of the house with his friends, only to return late in the night. Every other day Anu would try hard to find the man she had fallen in love with, the man she had married, the man she had spent her time with in Bali, the man who had loved her once like a hopeless romantic. The lucky days on which she used to get a glace of that man, it would vanish as quickly as it came. There were no more romantic dates, no more movie nights, and very occasional private dinners.

"They won't like it Anu, the elders in my family."

"Like what Karan? We are married. Why can't you and I spend our Sunday evening the way we want? In private. We live in this house with everyone, once a week, we can go out for a few hours na, just you and me to spend some quality time." Anu tried to share her heart with her husband.

"You're not getting it Anu, I cannot tell my family members I am taking my wife out on a date. Earlier it was different, you were not my wife or a member of this house."

"As your wife, now I have more right to go out with you Karan."

"Goodnight Anu, I don't want to talk about this anymore." That night, for the first time, Anu had feared for her future in this marriage.

&

"Karan, why have you changed so much since our marriage?" One night, Anu asked her husband who was busy playing some games on his phone.

Silence. There was no reply.

"Karan, do you even love me anymore?" This time she came near to her husband and kept her head on his shoulder.

"I don't know." He replied this time, his eyes still fixed on the screen.

"Have I made any mistake?" She asked again, tears visible in her eyes

"Mistake, Anu, a mistake is singular... because of you I have become the laughing stock of the whole family." He replied in a sarcastic tone, his attention still on the game.

"What are you saying, Karan?

"Yes, you couldn't become the kind of daughter-in-law my family wanted, needed. Everyone keeps on taunting me, that it was my foolishness to choose you over so many other deserving girls."

"Excuse me?" Anu raised her face from his shoulders and eyed him.

"You're selfish Anu, you bring so much sadness in my family, all this nonsense of being an educated, independent, feminist, and modern woman of yours has destroyed my family life. I should have listened to my friends about not marrying a feminist. They had warned me that feminists don't become good wives and daughters-in-law and mothers, that they don't obey the rules neither do they fulfill their womanly duties, but always demand equality and freedom like men. I should've listened to them, but love had blinded me." Anu was feeling like someone had just stabbed her in her heart.

"Having opinions, making some decisions of my life, not giving up on my parents or my choices or identity is nonsense for you Karan?"

"Yes, it is absolute nonsense for me. Why do you always have to be the flag bearer of this gender equality? Can't you just behave as normal Indian women do? Normal Indian women are expected to keep their husband and husband's family above everything for centuries, everything else should come secondary for them, that's how it has always been, and these women are the true women who deserve marriage. Not women like you who cannot change themselves for their marriage."

"I cannot be the kind of woman who can simply live life like a sheep, in total control of someone else."

"Then you know what Anu, just forget about getting any love or respect from me as well."

"For gaining your love, I have to kill myself?" She asked, her voice breaking.

"No. You just have to follow whatever I and my family asks you to do. You become the kind of wife and daughter-in-law we want, and you'll get what you deserve, our love, respect and acceptance." He answered.

"Which is in nothing else other than living in this house for the rest of my life without any voice, opinion, and freedom." She curtly replied, but Karan didn't answer.

"Well then, I think that's the deal I am willing to pass." She murmured, switched off the lamp, and went to sleep without throwing any look at Karan.

Few more months passed, but the things were the same. The distance was growing between Karan and Anu, and other than the occasional needful sexual activity and some random conversations, most of their time together was spent in heated arguments. When alone, Anu often used to think about how much her love story had failed in comparison to the time they had started dating. To save her marriage, Anu did exactly what most women do in such a scenario, she turned to her mother for advice.

"Don't worry beta, it will get better. I am sure. In the early years, every marriage is a bit difficult. You are getting to know him and his family, they are all getting to know you. Just treat them like you do with us. Always remember, a woman has to sacrifice more to keep the marriage going smoothly in Indian society. I think you both should plan a baby, a lot of things fall into place after having a baby." Her mother was a simple lady, submissive to her father, and while growing up, Anu had promised herself that she would never leave her self respect to save her marriage. It was exactly why she had studied and worked hard, bagged a job, to become financially independent. When she had met Karan, she had thought him to be someone who will consider her as an equal. That was why she had agreed to date him, be in a relationship with him, and finally say yes to him for marriage, even though they come from drastic cultures, she somehow knew that they would be able to make it work, but now, it was looking like a far fetched dream. Talking to her mother had yielded the same result as the conversation with Karan did.

One fine day, when Anu woke up, she rushed to the washroom and threw up instantly. Her head was feeling extremely light and she clutched on the tap to save herself from falling.

"What happened, are you okay?" Karan came rushing after hearing her vomit twice.

"I don't know, I am not feeling well." She said in a dizzy voice.

"Come, lie down on the bed." He scooped her up in his arms and walked up to bed. She blushed on seeing his care. In times like these, she always chided herself for doubting Karan and his love for her. Yes, they were having issues, but which married couple doesn't have their own set of issues? She, at that moment, knew that they could work it all out.

"Did you eat something bad?" He asked.

"No."

"You want me to take you to a doctor?"

It was then it suddenly hit Anu.

"I don't think so. Karan, can you run-up to the medical store and get me two pregnancy test kits? Bring two different brands."

Karan's eyes widened.

"You think?" He exhaled deeply.

Anu nodded. "Come to think of it, I haven't gotten my periods in more than two months. I just didn't realize in all the tensions. We might be pregnant." She added.

Karan nodded, patted her cheek, and rushed out. He was back in fifteen minutes with two pregnancy kits. "Why two different brands?" He handed her the kits and questioned curiously.

"Just to be double sure." She answered as went inside the washroom.

Karan was sitting on the bed, his heart pounding, feeling as if it will come out of his mouth and fall.

After five minutes when Anu finally came out, he looked at her like he was a student desperately waiting for his result to be announced.

"We are going to be parents." Anu finally unveiled the secret and broke down in happy tears.

"Anu? I am going to be a father?" He jumped with joy too.

"Yes, yes, yes. We are going to be parents." She hugged him, and he hugged her back with intense warmth.

Maybe her mother was right. Maybe having a baby will, after all, bring them closer. At that moment, Anu was hoping for the very best.

It was all she had to keep going.

Things were looking bright. Instead of finding faults in everything Anu did, her family members were treating her with care, and utmost priority was being given to her food and health. Even for little things, she was surrounded by one or the other at her beck and call.

"Arey Anu, why are you climbing such steep stairs? I would have gone to the terrace to bring clothes. Go and take a rest. Call someone if you need anything." Her mother-in-law would say if Anu even tried to do some household work.

"Bhabhi, here, a steaming hot plate of noodles. You love them na?" Her younger sister-in-law would say almost every other evening, serving her some lip-smacking snacks right in her room. However, the best part wasn't just the lovely behavior of all the family members, but the newly found affection she was receiving from Karan.

"Did you eat your medicines?" He would message her ten times a day from the office.

"Yes, don't worry." She would reply.

He would take a half-day leave every time she needed to visit the doctor for her checkup. He would bring her flowers and chocolates, he would watch her favorite movies with her. He was trying hard to keep her happy in her pregnancy, and such affection brought them both a lot closer. Anu was beginning to fall in love with her baby.

Anu, for the first time after her marriage, was truly happy in her new home with her new family. She finally felt accepted and a treasured member of the family, finally felt that she belonged in that clan. This was the feeling she had been craving for since the day she entered that home. Anyways, what does an average Indian girl want? To feel loved, respected, and accepted in the family of her husband, after all, she had left everything of hers behind to join them, and she was now getting her rightful place in the family.

Things were looking bright to Anu, but her hopes were again short-lived.

"Anu, my parents and grandparents are thinking about conducting a Havan in our home for our baby." Anu had received a message from Karan one Tuesday afternoon.

"That's great Karan." She typed back.

"Yes. Also, there are certain things you ought to do from now on, given you're entering the fifth month of your pregnancy." She received his reply after a few minutes.

"Certain things like?"

Suddenly her phone started ringing. It was Karan.

"Yes mister, tell me." She picked up the call in a cheerful manner.

" Anu, I was wanting to tell you this since last month, but I didn't know how would you react, so I postponed it. But now I cannot anymore."

"Then tell me what is it?" She assured him lovingly.

"It is kind of a tradition in our family that the firstborn of every son should be a male child. My grandfather, my father, my uncles, my brother's, everyone had a boy first. It's auspicious for us, as a blessing for many generations. So now it is our turn to give my family a male child. And they want to keep this Havan for the same."

Anu for once thought she had misheard.

"I am sorry Karan, I didn't understand. Maybe I heard something wrong."

But when Karan repeated his words, leaving no scope of getting it wrong, and it made Anu furious.

"What the hell Karan, are you out of your mind? What does it even mean that we need to have a baby boy to uphold some sort of coincidental tradition of your home? Sons having baby boys as their firstborn till now was a pure coincidence. Nothing more."

"Calm down Anu."

"No, I will not calm down. This is our baby we are talking about, how does it even matter if it's a boy or a girl, it's our baby. I would be happy if this havan is kept for the health of our baby, instead of carrying out for a baby boy."

"It doesn't matter what you or I think. It's a family tradition and has happened for decades. The firstborn of every son has been a son for many generations and my family believes that this havan will ensure that this tradition isn't broken."

Anu was visibly and audibly on fire by now.

"How can you be so stupid? You and I are educated, people. We know that the gender of the baby isn't determined by these things."

"The havan will happen Anu, you don't get an option in this," Karan shouted in anger and disconnected the phone.

The havan did happen, however, it wasn't a success as after four months, Anu delivered a baby girl, somehow breaking the very 'tradition' of the family.

XV

Humans are selfish and they respond well only to circumstances that are favorable to them, they're only happy and adjusting in situations that go according to their plan, and when the time becomes adverse, only the strongest, most mature, and intelligent make it out as a winner, the rest of them simply drowning in an ocean of their miserable life, blaming others.

Anu and her in-laws were feeling exactly like that, both parties blaming each other for destroying their hope of having good times.

Karan and his family would often indirectly blame her for breaking the age-old tradition of having a son as the firstborn. Anu kept on blaming them for being obnoxiously orthodox and sexist. The tensions in the house were invariably rising and all the love Anu was getting in her pregnancy was retracted after Kia's birth.

"Karan, I want to go and live with my parents for some time. I am leaving tomorrow with Kia."

It was Saturday and Karan was reading a magazine. Kia, who was lying just beside him was throwing her hands and legs at him as if asking for her father's love and attention, but in the three months of her birth, she rarely got what was her right. Anu picked up Kia and gently kissed her, and then looked at Karan waiting for an answer.

"Karan, I said something."

"Yes, I heard it. You can go if you want to. I'll drop you at the station." He replied in a dry tone.

Anu kept Kia back down on the bed and silently took out a suitcase. She neatly packed all the stuff she would be needing for the upcoming months. She kept her bank statements and debit cards. There was no point in burdening her parents financially more than what was necessary. What she was going to do, what was in her heart, Anu had no idea. All she knew at that time was that she needed to breathe freely away from Karan and his family, else she was sure a nervous breakdown was just around the corner for her.

She had tried hard for almost two years to be a part of this family, and she was sure that Karan and his family must have tried to work out things in their ways, but somewhere she had understood the fact they all wanted her to completely change herself and become submissive to their conservative patriarchal ways of life, and that was something too huge for her to simply say yes to.

By evening, her two suitcases were packed. Karan was watching her preparations from the corner of his eyes but was silent. It was evident that Anu wasn't going to her parent's home for a few days or weeks, but maybe for several months. But he still chose to remain silent. "It would be nice to live alone for some time." He thought to himself. It wasn't like Karan didn't love his wife or daughter. He did. But the point wasn't about love. First Anu and her actions had demeaned him in front of his family. Before marriage, he knew how much he had to convince the entire clan to say yes for Anu. He thought that by being a perfect daughter-in-law, she would make him proud in front of his folks, that would prove it to them that she was the right choice made by him, that she could be the daughter-in-law and wife they had wanted for their family, but she did the exact opposite by becoming an empowered woman and wife in his orthodox patriarchal family. But when she became pregnant, he finally had hopes of giving another firstborn as son according to the family tradition and save his face, but Kia came and just like her mother, pulled him down.

"When will you come back?" He finally asked Anu, after dinner while she was feeding Kia.

"I don't know Karan. I think I might take some time. I am tired, really tired." She answered, still looking at Kia.

"Very well, I understand." Karan had wanted to say something more, but then he changed his mind. The next day, Anu was back in her maternal home, and now it was time for her to make some decisions for her and her daughter's future.

XVI

The first few weeks were like a breath of fresh air for Anu. The days were relaxed and lazy, and the nights brought deep untroubled sleep. She was away from all the taunts or the judgmental looks, from all the stress and pressures. She was with her people, and there wasn't any fear of offending someone with her actions. She was feeling free. Her mother was treating her with delicious delicacies, her father was pampering Kia with different kinds of toys, and outing on every weekend with her younger sister was becoming her favorite part of the week. She was with her people after a year, and only by being in her maternal house with her own blood family, Anu was beginning to realize how caged her life was in Karan's home.

Karan.

In the three weeks, she and Kia had been away from Karan, he had only called them thrice, asking about their well being, if they need money for anything, and when they're coming back, but in none of the calls she felt the urgency, the love, the care or the longing in his voice for his wife and daughter.

"How are you doing Karan?"

Anu was reading a book, and everyone else in the home was sleeping. It was a lazy, weekend noon of summer, and suddenly, Anu was missing her husband, so she decided to text him. She had typed in the message, sent it, but there was no reply, even when he was online.

"Maybe he's busy in something, he'll reply in a few minutes." She thought and kept her phone aside, resuming her reading, and after a few minutes, she dozed off beside her baby, drifting apart into a world of dreams, totally forgetting about her text to Karan.

Anu woke up after two hours when her sister brought a cup of tea.

"Wake up Di."

Anu sat up straight in her bed and turned to look at her daughter, but found her missing.

"She's with papa. He's playing with her. She got up an hour back and he took her so that you can rest peacefully."

"Acha," Anu uttered mindlessly and picked up her phone to check any new messages from Karan but was extremely disappointed to find no reply. He hadn't even seen the message. She picked the cup of steaming tea and dialed Karan's number. It rang ten times, but the call wasn't picked. She called him again, but even the second time, the call wasn't connected. She threw her phone on the other side in disappointment. She had given her marriage a thought, but how can a marriage survive when only one person is trying to salvage it.

Anu waited for an hour desperately for Karan to return the calls or messages, but when none of it happened, she dialed her mother-in-law's number. "Hello, Anu."

"Hello mummy, how are you?"

"I am good. How are you, how's Kia?" She asked.

"We both are doing fine."

"So when are you coming back? It's almost going to be a month. You should come back now." Though Anu was on the other side of the audio call, she could hear her mother-in-law frowning. She knew she had been the talk of the house in her absence, and not in a good way, not that she cared about what they all talked about her behind her back. "Mummy I will come back in a few days." Anu lied to divert the conversation, "Where is Karan? I am messaging and calling him for hours now. He's not replying. Is he okay?"

"Did he not tell you?"

"Tell me what?"

"Arey he has gone for a weekend trip to Jaipur with his friends."

"When?"

"Today, in the morning. He'll be back by tomorrow night."

"Ohh."

"Didn't he tell you? You're his wife and your husband didn't tell you what he is upto?" Anu could feel the mockery in her mother-in-law's voice, but she let it pass.

"Ohh yes, he did mention. These days Kia keeps me so busy, I completely forgot."

"Then you should make sure that you remember everything your husband says." She instructed.

"Yes. I'll keep that in mind. Alright, Kia is crying Mom, I'll talk to you later. Bye!" Anu disconnected the call, without waiting for her reply. Her eyes were watering and she was in no mood to talk to anyone any longer. Karan went for a weekend getaway and didn't even feel it necessary to tell her. Just then, her phone rang. It was Karan.

"So you don't think it's important to tell your wife that you're going out somewhere with your friends for a few days?" She asked directly, fuming in anger.

"I called you to tell you about it now."

"Ohh, once you've planned everything, arranged for everything, already left home, already have reached there, after doing all of this, you remembered that you should let me know at the last. How thoughtful and responsible of you Karan."

"You know what's your problem Anu? You just want to dominate my life around. You always forget I am the husband between the two of us. Because you wanted to simply go and stay at your parent's place for months, you did, didn't even think about what all would I have to listen because of you back at home." His tone was as bitter as hers.

"So? Just because you're the husband, or your family is taunting you because of me, you get the liberty to do and go anywhere you want to relax without even informing me?"

"Just get lost Anu, you've ruined my life. Every time I talk to you, I suffer a headache. You've killed all my happiness."

"Likewise, Karan, marrying you was the worst ever decision I made. At least we both agree that this marriage was a huge blunder."

"So why don't you just leave?" He shouted like a wild man.

"You know what. That's what I'll do. I am not coming back to you ever, and neither is Kia. Enjoy your trip!"

And then she threw the phone, breaking it into pieces, the phone becoming a replica of her marriage.

XVII

Two months later. Anu's maternal house. Karan and his parents were sitting in the living room. In front of them, Anu was sitting with Kia in her lap, in between her parents. Her younger sister brought tea and snacks for all of them.

"Anu, what is this behavior? Why aren't you coming back?" Karan's mother asked.

Anu remained silent,but looked at her father. He nodded gently.

"Mummy, don't you know why am I not?"

"No, she doesn't know, and neither do I." This time it was Karan.

"I don't want to live with you, Karan. I don't want to be in this marriage. I am deeply unhappy."

Karan and his parents looked disappointed. They were not expecting that. No daughter-in-law in the entire family has ever behaved like Anu did from the first day of her marriage. Her waking time was seven in the morning instead of five, her eating habits were different, she used to sit inside her room for hours on end, frequent visits to her maternal house, not changing her name after marriage, going out alone with their son for outings, they had tolerated her odd behavior for years, only for the sake of family's name and to save their son's marriage. But now, this girl wants a divorce? Karan's parents looked at him, as if wanting to tell him from their eyes, "We told you so, she can never be the right choice for our family." But now, as his parents, it was their duty to save his home from falling apart. "I don't know what you have taken to heart? We all have always tried our best to keep you happy." This time, it was her father-in-law.

"Yes Papa, I am not denying. You all treat me the way most in-laws treat daughters-in-law in this country. And I won't be partial, I treat you all just the way most daughters-in-law treat their in-laws in India. But then, I don't think any of us is happy, or even comfortable in this sort of arrangement." Anu managed to utter these words despite being filled with emotional turmoil.

"You want to break our marriage?" Karan asked her, and for a second, she heard the pain in it and not shock.

"Don't you want it too? I and my daughter are just a burden for you, aren't we? Always pulling you down in front of your family? Did you even ever considered us both as a part of your family Karan? No, for you, we were always outsiders, I was an outsider for you all, maybe still am, and I don't feel I can live like that, and even if I can, I cannot let my daughter go through any pain." This time, Anu was directly addressing Karan, confronting him.

There was pin-drop silence in the room like no one else existed apart from Karan and Anu, both looking into each other's eyes with a look of disappointment and betrayal. "I have always regarded you as a part of my family. In two years of marriage, did I only give you pain and sadness Anu? Can you say for sure I don't love my daughter?"

"Yes you gave me happiness, a lot of it, but you gave me pain as well, just like I must have given you."

"I have made mistakes Anu, and so have you, and so have my family, because all of us are humans, we are not perfect, none of us is. I have a large joint family, and when we all live together with lots of people, differences arise. Yes, you're not the kind of wife or daughter-in-law we wanted, and I am not the husband or my family is not the kind of in-laws you expected, but no one here is a bad or evil person, we are all misfit."

Anu was silent this time, and so was everyone else.

"I won't justify anything Anu, I can only say that I want you both in my life, you both are important to me. I promise I'll try to become a better husband and father this time."

Anu looked at her parents.

"Anu, beta this is your life, your decision. We won't influence your decision, but remember that if you like, you can live with us here. It's your home and will always be." Anu's father held his daughter's hand reassuringly and said the words out loud for everyone to hear.

Anu smiled and thanked her father with her eyes. Only a daughter can understand the importance of having her parent's support after her marriage in a society where a daughter is not considered as a part of the family she was born and bred in after her marriage and is often pressurized to adjust and sacrifice even at the cost of her identity and self-respect in her marital home by her parents.

"Karan, I appreciate your words and feelings, but I come from a nuclear family. I tried hard for two years to adjust to your large and conservative joint family, but I don't think I can do it anymore. Why do I need someone's permission to do a simple job? Why do I need someone's permission to visit my parents for a few days? Why did everyone expect my firstborn to be a boy? Why do I need to always follow a set of rules and regulations regarding clothing, eating, talking, sleeping, waking? I did not sign up for admission to some military school when I was marrying you. I was okay about little adjustments here and there that comes with every family, but the environment of your house has made me lose myself. I no longer recognize the woman I have become in two years." They all were listening to her, giving her space to speak her mind. She resumed.

"I get it that even they're adjusting with me as much as they can, maybe it's not their fault even, we are very different people, and all of us have tried hard to live under one roof for years, and it's not working out, especially for me. You are all one team, I feel alone there."

"You don't want to live with me Anu?"

"Maybe I do Karan, but I am not ready for being caged in your love, or remain confined in your house, maintaining a list of rules to make you all happy at the cost of my own identity, individuality, and freedom. I cannot do that. I am sorry."

"And what if I say that you don't have to live there?"

Anu was surprised.

"What do you mean?"

"Remember that job in Mumbai I told you about? Earlier I did not want to take it up, but now I have said yes to it. I think it would be good for the three of us to spend some years alone. Start our life again?"

Anu was now struggling to comprehend Karan's words. Was he talking about moving away from his family and settling into a new city? But how? When earlier Anu had requested him to do so, every time she had been called as a home breaker. But now, he was taking this decision, how?

"I will be leaving for Mumbai next month, by then, do think about our relationship again. Kia needs both of us

Anu, don't forget that. I'll wait for your call."

Karan stood up and touched Anu's parent's feet. He then turned to Kia and kissed her on her forehead. Then he turned towards his parents, signaling them that it was time to go back.

"Bhai Sahab, these two are still kids, they don't know much about marriages and families, but we are elders and we must ensure that their marriage, their home, and their future doesn't fall apart. In normal circumstances, we must have never allowed Karan to leave his family and go settle in a new city with his wife and child, but just for the sake of these three, we are even ready for that. Now we can only expect that you'll do the same for your daughter's and granddaughter's life."

After a few minutes of farewell formalities, Karan and his parents had left for their home, leaving Anu behind deep in her newly perplexed mind.

"Karan, can we keep this bean bag in here?"

"Sure."

"And how about putting up a little swing in the balcony?"

"You want to have a swing?"

"Yes. I will order one from Amazon."

"Alright. If it makes my wife happy, then I have got no problem in that."

"Really?" She felt her heart dancing.

"Yes. It's our home, it's your home. Decorate it just the way you want."

Karan planted a gentle kiss on Anu's lips, and she could sense the love with a tinge of lust in his body. She snuggled deep into his arms. Her decision about giving her marriage a second chance was turning out to be pretty good. In the two weeks, they had spent in Mumbai, in their new flat and new life, she had noticed a drastic change in Karan's behavior towards herself and Kia. Maybe the pressure of being a perfect son, grandson, brother, uncle was less on him, who knows? Yes, she was feeling bad about what had happened. She had never wanted to be the girl who would be called the 'home breaker', and for two years she tried.

Even when she failed, she chose to end the marriage instead of asking him to move out. But then, he decided to start a nuclear family, and she had agreed because of Kia, and also because she still loved him. She had belived that their marriage deserved another chance, that Kia deserved the love of both her parents. "Don't worry Karan, we will go back to our home in a few years, once you and I sort out all the differences between us, we will surely go back to the place we belong." She assured him, thankful, for she knew that Karan had indeed made a great sacrifice for her.

"Hmm. Chalo I am getting late for work now. Will see you in the evening."

Karan quickly picked up Kia who was busy rolling on the floor, kissed her on her forehead, put her back on the floor, and waved bye to both of them.

"Don't forget to text me when you reach your office."

"Okay," Karan shouted from the corridor, and then, Anu heard the sound of the lift door closing.

"Papa is gone Kia, now Mumma and Kia will go and have a warm bath with bubbles, then we will have some fruits, and then Kia will go to sleep and Mumma will wash all the dirty clothes." Anu picked up Kia, talking with her in a toddler's voice, simultaneously picking up all the toys Kia had scattered around the house, all the while Kia making faces at her mother and giggling out loud when her mother reciprocated her actions. Though late, but Anu was living her fairytale finally.

XIX

The first six months in Mumbai were lovely for Anu. She was feeling free; she was feeling like a new bride. Cooking her recipes, decorating her home with her style, wearing comfortable pajamas in her home, watching late night movies with Karan, or making love with him in the hall on the couch without any fear, she was loving her life, and if she was correct, Karan was enjoying it too, though he wasn't as vocal about it like her because of guilt. Kia was growing up, learning new things. Anu and Karan had admitted her into a nearby playschool, where every day she learned something, and then she came back and told whatever it was to her mother, and then to her father later in the evening.

"She's learning things very quickly." Anu kept the coffee mug on the table and sat down on the bed, instantly feeling relaxed after a direful day.

Karan simply nodded and picked up his mug.

"What is it, Karan? You're looking lost for a few days."

"It's nothing."

"You're my husband, I love you, and I know something is troubling you. Tell me what is it?"

"I am missing my family Anu, I have been a bad son, I broke that family. You know, no son has ever moved out like this, leaving his family behind for his wife."

"I know that Karan, and we will go back, by next year. You can put an application in your company for transfer to Delhi. I am sure by this time, next year, we will be back with everyone else."

"This was a mistake Anu. Coming here was a mistake."

"No Karan, it was not a mistake. Just see how much we have bonded in the last six months. We have cooked together, we have slept till noon, we have made love on the balcony on a full moon night, we have danced in the hall, we have come home late after a long drive, we have shared laughs, we have talked about our issues and we have solved them. I have understood you so much better than before."

Karan kept silent and after a moment looked at Anu.

"You. It's all because of you."

"Me? What are you saying?" There was a thud in Anu's heart.

"You separated me from my family. It was you who wanted all this."

"No Karan, I didn't ask you to move to Mumbai or take up this job. I asked for a divorce because our marriage was only making all of us unhappy."

Karan threw the mug on the floor in anger.

"Yes, because you never wanted to make any changes or adjustments in your behavior. Just hear yourself Anu, you were willing to divorce me instead of changing your attitude. You know Anu, I loved you enough, so much that I got ready to do something no son has ever done in my family, I left them all because I wanted to be with you. They loved me enough to let me go just because they wanted to see me in my marriage, but you, you couldn't make a few changes in yourself. For you, nothing of this has been ever important."

"Don't behave like a maniac Karan. I tried for two years, but we all are so different from each other that things went for a toss. Yes, I asked for a divorce because I never wanted to break a family, but then you asked me to give another chance to our marriage in a new city."

"And like a selfish woman you took it, instead of telling me that you would instead try harder to please everyone and live there."

Anu was trying hard to control her anger because she knew that it won't give any fruitful results if both of them would behave angrily.

"No Karan, I didn't tell you that because I wanted to live with you alone for a year or two. I wanted us to understand each other better as husband and wife, as parents of Kia, and two years would have been enough in making our bond strong enough. Then we would have gone back."

"Just keep quiet. I don't want the stupid explanations, you did all this Anu, and I will never forgive you for doing this. For me, you'll always be the culprit of my family. You couldn't adjust to them, so you made me sacrifice my happiness. You made me abandon my family and for that, I won't ever forgive you."

XX

All the dreams Anu were starting to see again were being shattered. In the initial months, Anu had seen a silver lining in her marriage. She had thought that maybe after a bumpy and rough start, her marriage could finally leave the bad times behind and convert itself into something cordial and meaningful, but once again, she was beginning to see the old toxic cycles, and this time, she knew there was no one else to blame apart from herself and Karan.

Was it her and Karan from the beginning? Were they both to be blamed for their failing marriage instead of their families? There was no one else in their home at the moment who could be blamed for creating any misunderstanding or tension between them. And if they couldn't be happy even when they were just alone in a house, if they were finding it difficult to lead a happy life together, maybe the problem was inside them. Back home, at least she had an excuse, blame Karan's family for her marriage, but here, no one was controlling their lives, still, things were getting messier every day. Karan was ignoring her out of anger and in response; she had started to blame every single thing on him. "I'll talk with Karan once he comes back. If it's not going to work out in Mumbai, it would be better to move back to Delhi." She murmured to herself.

That night, Karan came back at two in the morning, heavily drunk. "Helloooo... Hi Anu... Sorry goott late, friends took me tooooo a partyyy, and it wassss awesomenee." Karan almost sang and fell on the couch.

"Karan, I had been calling you for hours. Do you have any idea how tensed I was?" Anu was fuming in anger.

"Shhh, don't you dare shhhoouutt on mee."

"Why are you behaving like this Karan? What's wrong with you?"

"You knoww what? I appliedd foor a transfeeerrr back to Delhiii, but they rejected ittt. Now I would have to live here for twooo years, onlyy because of you." He blurted in almost unfathomable language.

Anu sat beside him and took a long breath. These days, half of her energy was being consumed in controlling her anger. What good would have to show it done? What would Kia feel after seeing both her parents shouting at the top of their lungs? Confusion? Fear? Terror?

"I am sorry Karan. But what can we do now? This time will pass quickly, sooner than you think." She held her husband's hand and spoke lovingly.

"Don't talk with me and go from here." Karan pushed her hand away.

Anu kept on looking at her drunken husband, who within few moments passed out on the couch. She wiped tears from her eyes, pulled up Karan's feet on the couch, and wrapped a blanket over him. Instead of going inside their bedroom where Kia was sleeping, Anu went in the balcony, sat down on the floor, and stared up at the sky. Might be she was waiting for the new day and sun to arrive, in the world, as well as in her life. She was tired of living in the constant dark.

XXI

In the next few months, Anu was beginning to realize one fact: her marriage was slowly on the path of meeting a dead end, and by the pace, things were happening, the end was near. No matter how hard she was trying to set things right, there were absolutely no efforts or interest being shown from Karan's side. She would cook his favorite dish, he would come back home after having dinner with his colleagues. She would plan a silent and romantic movie and a pizza night with him, he would sleep way too early on the pretext of having some sort of sickness. All her questions would be answered in monosyllables and all her romantic gestures would be brushed off as drama. "Karan, what is up with you?" One Sunday she finally asked when he was watching some video on his phone.

"What do you mean?" He replied without looking at her.

"Are you not happy?"

"I am fine."

"No Karan, I asked you if you're happy or not."

"Yes, I am very happy."

Karan got up, plugged his phone in the charger, and went inside the bathroom to take a shower. Anu waited for him to say something, anything. Maybe even ask for a

"

towel or a soap. Nothing. After waiting for a few moments, she resumed her work of dusting and cleaning the entire mess in the bedroom. She was changing the bedsheet when Karan's phone started ringing. At first, she didn't pay any attention, but when the ringing stopped and the phone started buzzing for the notification sounds continuously, her curiosity got the better of her. She picked up his phone and unlocked it.

"Woah. Twenty messages from Ritu."

"Hey, keep my phone back." Just as Anu was going to open and read the messages, Karan came out from the bathroom. He was visibly shaken on seeing his phone in Anu's hands. He almost ran across the room and snatched his phone back from her hand.

"Were you spying on me Anu?" He snapped.

"No Karan. Your phone was buzzing rigorously; I was just checking who is calling. Why will I spy on you?"

"Why were you checking who is calling or texting me?"

Anu glared at her husband.

"What is wrong with you? What kind of conversation is this? I cannot see who is calling or messaging my husband twenty times on a Sunday and regarding what? I am not spying, but that doesn't mean I don't have the right to know what's going in your life."

"Whatever Anu, just don't touch my phone."

"Who is this Ritu by the way?"

"A colleague."

Anu watched Karan as he put on his track pants and a white tee shirt.

"Colleagues call and message these many times on a weekend?"

"Are you doubting me?"

"No, I am just asking."

"You're asking me in doubt, not casually."

"Alright Karan, I have work to do, so I won't bother picking up a fight with you."

"Then go. I would be more than happy if you'll just leave me alone."

"If things will continue like this, then maybe soon I'll leave you alone Karan."

"What did you say?" Karan came near her and shouted in a way that sent shivers down Anu's spine. She had never seen Karan this angry. He came nearer, his eyes red with anger, his facial muscles tightening, and before Anu could have reacted, she felt his hand hard across her face, losing her balance and instantly falling on the floor.

"You will leave me? You? I'll destroy you if you'll ever say that again in my house." When Karan had left the room in anger and Anu had stood up on her feet and looked at herself in the mirror, she could still see the redness of his slap on her cheek.

Little did she know that it was the beginning of the end.

XXII

Anu woke up from her nightmare in a shock. She sat down, her breaths fast and shallow. She touched her cheeks, they were wet. She had been crying all along in her dreams the complete night, remembering all details from her marriage. It had failed, it had all failed. From the day she met Karan, or from the day she decided to marry him, or from the day she married him, or from the day she started living in his home, or from the day she delivered a baby girl, or from the day they moved to Mumbai, or from the day she suspected he was cheating on her, or from the day he had first slapped her, or at the time she came to know that he had gone out for a weekend with another woman, Anu didn't know exactly at what point did her marriage fell apart, but she did have the intelligence and courage to admit that her marriage had indeed crumbled into pieces and that she couldn't stay with Karan any more because if she did, she will lose herself forever.

She picked up her phone to check the time. It was five in the morning, and there was one missed call from Karan at 1:00 A.M. She unlocked the phone and found one message from him as well, which stated that he would be home by the next evening and that he will take her and Kia to a

"

movie and then they will have dinner at her favorite Chinese restaurant. He also said that he was sorry for his behavior and that he loved her.

Anu laughed bitterly at the message that offered her a consolation prize and fake proclamations of love from her cheating husband. She got up, went to the bathroom, and washed her face. After freshening up, she made some coffee for herself, picked up the writing pad, a pen, and sat down to write a letter.

"Dear I

No, no dear for you, maybe you no longer deserve it. Karan, I still remember the first time I had met you, and until now, I regarded it as one of the most special events of my life, but not anymore. I now think that meeting you, falling in love with you, marrying you, and giving you another chance, all of it was some of the biggest mistakes of my life, but not anymore.

You know what Karan, ever since the day we both got married and I moved into your home, I had always blamed your family for our bad marriage. I always felt, like most other wives that it was your family who was coming in between our relationship. But now when I look back, I realize how wrong I was. It was not them, it was never them. It was always you. You failed to be both, a good son and a good husband. You kept on treating all of us as different units, you never made me and your family feels like one unit. And then you kept on blaming me when it was you who failed to become a bridge between us. It was your duty to connect all of us as a son and a husband, but for you, I was always an outsider from whom your family needed protection. My actions became a parameter for your false ego.

Karan, a man is as much responsible for a marriage and a home as a woman. Not more, not less, and when a woman comes with a man to his home after marrying him, it's his responsibility to connect his former family of older relationships with the new family he is creating with his wife and children.

But you failed in it badly, and always blamed me for your failures, and like a fool, I accepted all your accusations, thinking that you must be right and the fault indeed lies in me or your family. But now I know the truth.

It was always you, the fault was in you, and it still is. In Mumbai, there was no one between us, but even then, look at what you did. You again blamed me for breaking your family, when the decision of staying away was made by you, and that too for a few years. But no, again, instead of talking it out like mature adults, you chose to turn violent and abusive, forced me to have sex even when I said no, manipulated me into having another child, shattering my confidence, refusing me for a career, but even after all this, a part of me wanted to be with you because I loved you, but today, all my hopes regarding this marriage have been broken, when I came to know that you are cheating on me with another woman. As I said, it was you, who was majorly the problem, not them, not me, and it is primarily because of you that our marriage fell apart. Instead of making a team with me and working on this marriage and having a complete one family, you always blamed me and stood against me, like this marriage was just my responsibility, like making you happy always should have been my only motive, whereas you looked for the easy things. You slapped me, abused me, cheated on me, you told me I couldn't do a job, blamed me for having a daughter, or that I don't deserve a vacation, you made me doubt myself, my abilities, my mental and emotional health. Because of you, I suffered for years.

But not anymore, as I can now see how toxic of a person you're especially for me.

I am leaving you; Karan, forever, and I won't come back to you.

No point in escalating this or intimidating me, because if you try to pull off any cheap stunts, I'll show you what I am willing to do to get my respect, happiness, and life back.

Have a good life. Goodbye."

Anu folded the paper carefully and kept it in Karan's study where she was sure it will gather his attention almost instantly. She felt extremely light, even after knowing that she was cheated, that she was abused, that her marriage had crumbled apart, more than any sadness, she felt free like she was getting out of a dark prison after a lifetime.

She packed her bags, woke up Kia, got her dressed, called a cab, and left her home without looking back even once. What's the point in being attached to something which was never hers.

Epilogue

After ten years.

"Mom, wake up, look what we have received in the mail.."

Anu was not sleeping, she was just lying with her eyes closed, thinking absolutely nothing. As a woman, the superpower of thinking nothing was a little hard for her to achieve, but by patience, she had finally learned the art to have a calm mind.

"Relax Kia. Take a breath first. I am not sleeping. Tell me what has happened?"

"Mom, just see this letter. It just arrived. It's from Tiger Publishers."

"What? Give it to me."

Kia handed over the letter to her mother, who tore the envelope and started reading it for seconds.

"What does it say, Mom?"

Anu kept the letter on the side table and hugged Kia tightly.

"Mom, what happened, tell me already."

"My book Kia, my book has been declared a bestseller, selling over one million copies in the past year."

Kia jumped with a mixed emotion of shock, surprise, excitement, and happiness.

"What? Really? Your book is a bestseller now?"

"Yes, yes, yes my baby. The book has been declared a bestseller, and the publisher company wants to sign a contract regarding the second book with a whopping advance of ten lakh rupees."

"Oh, I hear money, and when I hear money, I come around."

Anu and Kia looked at the door of the room and found Raman standing there with a pizza. Kia ran up to him and took the pizza box from his hand and then hopped on towards the kitchen.

"Careful Kid, and you Miss. Writer, I heard now you're a bestselling author of the country."

Anu blushed.

"Congratulation my love." He came closer and kissed Anu on the forehead.

"No, thank you, Raman, it's all because of you."

"No, it's you Anu. It is all your talent, your hard work, your dedication."

Anu smiled.

"Even you know why I am thanking you, Raman."

"No Anu, I don't know why you're thanking me now."

Anu held his hand in her hands.

"Thank you for everything that you have given me Raman because you have given me a lot. When I had first met you, three years after my divorce, I was as lost and lonely a woman could imagine; I was just torn, after what my ex-husband had done, not when I was married to him, but even when I asked for a separation, the kind of allegations he hurled at me, thank god I had mailed his cheating chats to myself before leaving, else he would have made everyone believed that it was me who was having an affair. That threat calls in nights, those constant fears that he'll take my baby away, for years I lived in constant fear. I had given up any hope of a good, normal life, forget about having a happy life."

She paused to wipe the moisture from her eyes. Raman's hand was still in hers, his eyes gleaming with a lot of emotions.

"But then, one day, in the NGO I had just joined to pass my time, I met you, and slowly, it was you who started making me feel alive again. It was because of you I started smiling for real, not the fake smile. You taught me to live life. You brought me out of the hell. You gave me hope that I could do so many things, write a book. You motivated me, you scolded me, you heard me whenever I wanted to vent out things, and those times when I simply wanted to scream and cry remembering the dark times, you silently held in your arms. You never attacked me for feeling sad or bad or showing my emotions, you simply gave me a natural safety net to be myself."

Raman kissed her on the forehead.

"I did all this because I loved you."

"No Raman, you didn't do this because you loved me, but because you respected me a woman and individual. That is why you took a stand for me when your family told you that they won't let you marry a divorcee, mother of a girl, also who is older than you by four years. You didn't abandon me for your family, or some other woman after making promises to me. You kept your words and you married me."

"And you won all their hearts by being the perfect daughter-in-law." He pulled Anu's cheeks.

"Because they're lovely people. Yes, initially there was ice, but because of your maturity, and efforts from all sides, things weren't that difficult to manage."

"I don't know why you're thanking me. I should be the one thanking you for coming into my life." He blushed.

Raman was leaning in to kiss Anu, but then suddenly they heard Kia.

"Mom, Aditya has woken up and looked at what he is doing on the walls. He's drawing a family picture of all of us."

Raman and Anu laughed and looked at each other. They both came out in the hall and saw their kids, Kia and Aditya playing with their two dogs, silver and cookie. It was a picture-perfect family moment.

"Thank you for giving me this beautiful family Anu. You always say that I have given you a lot, but in reality, it is you who have given me everything."

"Let's agree on a common fact, that we both are truly made for each other, and we are both thankful for this gift." Anu kissed her husband lightly on the lips.

"True." Raman smiled, kissed Anu's head, and pulled her into his warm embrace, both watching all their kids laughing and giggling freely.

ABOUT THE AUTHOR

Vidushi Gupta Loaded under the pressure to leave her mark, what could a CA Final cum MBA aspirant probably do in her life? Complete her professional degrees and start her career in the field she had been studying for the last five years? Probably not. As soon as she realized this is not what she wants to do, she took a U-turn towards her passion and started writing. Her journey started from blogs, then got into freelancing and finally turned towards writing fiction. Her love for words could be seen in every format of writing, be it short stories, articles, blogs, essays, poems, quotes and now a novel. She writes both in Hindi and English.

You can connect to her via her blog, website, or her social media handles where she loves to interact with her readers.

The Unending Maze

Amaya, a beautiful, young widow, who lost her husband Agastya to death two years back, slowly yet steadily finds color again in her life when she finds her solace in the mysterious Rehan. However, as the story unfolds, Amaya discovers that there is always a lot more going around her than what meets the eye, and she's in nothing but an unending maze with no way for her to escape. Who's Rehan? Is there any connection between Rehan and Agastya? What are Rehan's true motives? Set in the small town of Kalimpong in the Indian Himalayas, this romantic thriller has a shocking secret waiting to be unveiled.

Love, Relationship And Breakup: The Triangular Saga

In the all-new decade of the 2020s, the dating and love game will rise, hence giving even more space for romantic relationships to develop, and as much people would fall in the dating and relationship process, the more frequently breakups will take place, hence leaving the youth heartbroken, confused and skeptical about love, relationships, marriages, companionship and everything associated with them.

This short E-book is just a simple guide to give some insights about love, relationship, and breakup to the gen z so that they can make wise decisions when it comes to the matters of their heart.

The Three Tales

Rahul and Anjali have been trying hard for a baby, but one day, a medical report change the course of their lives.

What happens when the Mathur family moves in their new home and the daughter Shreya meets with a supernatural entity she cannot fight with?

Zarun and Sneha are in love with each other, but will their love break the shackles of society and religion and conquer it all?

"The Three Tales" is a collection of three short true incidences, where humans have used their positivity, courage, strength and hope to defeat some of the devilish demons of our society.

How to Write a Book: The Beginner's Guide

Do you aspire to become an author one day?

Writing is one of the best art forms, but at the same time, it is quite challenging too. Writing a book is a long journey, but with proper help and advice along the way can make a massive difference.

This short book is one such help on my behalf for all those who feel alone and confused in this journey.

Together, you and I can make world a beautiful book with our words, and what would be a better way than telling the world all the stories we have in our hearts, but to write down those stories, we all need a little push and help.

So here's one such push from me.

Happy Writing!

Shades of A Human: An Anthology

Humans show various emotions everyday, and it is the beauty of these emotions that truly make the stories around us beautiful. 'Shades Of A Human' is a collection of eleven short stories which captures various human emotions like love , anger, sadness, happiness, loss and many more. These are stories about humans and their lives.

Best Of Quora

Quora is one of the leading question-answers sites in the world as of today, and this short book comprises of some of my best and most upvoted answers of Quora during these years. Some of the answers are quacky and give some fun insights about both the genders, however, some other articles are the blunt truths of the Indian society in the twenty-first century that people need to embrace and accept and bring the necessary changes accordingly.

Romantic Games

Have you ever played the game of romance? Have you ever loved someone, but still got attracted to anyone else? Or have you been a character of such a story?

Based on the real-life incidents happening all around in this modern age, this short book talks about love, relationship, and infidelity in a crispy take.